SCAMPER'S
Hide-Away

BY
PATRICIA EYTCHESON TAYLOR

Scamper, the Mischievous Squirrel: Book 3

Scamper's Hide-Away
© 2011 Patricia Eytcheson Taylor

Published by:
Catch-A-Winner Publishing
PO Box 160125
San Antonio, TX 78280
Phone: 210-387-8189
E-mail: info@catchawinnerpublishing.com

ISBN: 978-0-9845630-3-6

Illustrator: Nancy Garnett Peterson

Other Books
by Patricia Eytcheson Taylor

Scamper with the Peanut Butter Feet
Hide and Seek with Scamper
Catch a Winner
Catch a Winner Leaves the Ranch
Catch a Winner and the Mystery Horse
Let's Ride a Texas Horse
On the Wings of the Wind: A Journey to Faith

To: Cole

Dedication

To all our grandchildren

Aunt Boo Says
Isn't Reading Fun!

Pat Eytcheson Taylor

An early cold chill in the air and the yellow leaves falling from the trees told Scamper, the big bushy-tailed squirrel, winter was just around the corner. Scamper wanted to find a warmer place to live.

Chip, the Chipmunk, Scamper's friend, was looking for his buried food. He could never remember where he buried it.

He had to rely on other animals or Scamper to help find his winter food.

Scamper was gathering pecans to take with him to his secret hide-away, but he would help Chip to have enough for the coming winter, too.

Chip wondered where this place was that Scamper was about to explore for his winter home. If it was way up high in the trees, Chip wasn't interested. He was a ground dweller.

Aunt Boo was busy working on her new laptop, sitting in the kitchen, where it was nice and warm inside the little house.

Shivering from the cold wind, Scamper sat on his favorite tree branch, looking in. This is what Scamper dreamed of, a nice warm and cozy place of his very own.

Scamper took
off to the
hole in the old
oak tree. Yes,
this is what
he wanted.

He slowly climbed into his present home,
and soon he was dreaming of that place,
the hide-away in Aunt Boo's house.

Aunt Boo had a rose trellis on the side of the house. Scamper used the rose trellis many times, climbing and running back and forth over the roof. He could always keep an eye on Aunt Boo from the rooftop as he enjoyed being high in the trees.

Today was Scamper's adventure to seek that hide-away place. There must be an opening somewhere to enter into Aunt Boo's warm and cozy house.

Scamper went around and around up on the roof. He peeked here and he peeked there. He peeked under the hanging eaves to see if there was a way to get into Aunt Boo's house.

Oh, oh, here it was. A cooling vent that led into the attic.

It was secured with metal strips nailed down to keep any intruders such as Scamper from entering.

It was now or never. The winter winds were getting colder and colder.

Scamper knew what had to be done. There was only one way. He had to use his sharp teeth and his sharp claws to make a hole big enough to squeeze through.

Scamper tugged and pulled with his teeth while his paws held onto the metal. Suddenly the metal gave way and Scamper pushed and wiggled his way through the hole. He found his hideaway in Aunt Boo's attic.

Scamper couldn't be happier. A beautiful blanket was lying on the floor, just for him to cuddle up in. He could play hide-and-seek with the spring coats hanging on a rack.

Suitcases stood open with old clothing to play in. There was a wreath with greens ready to be hung when Christmas came.

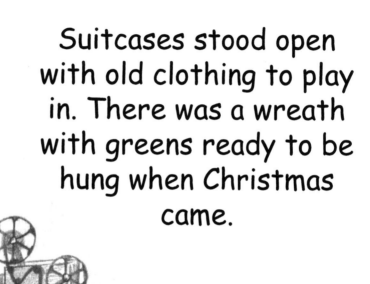

Scamper brought his pecans along, too. What more could a squirrel want? This was a perfect place to spend the winter.

Aunt Boo, with a big smile on her face, stirred the pot of soup on the stove. Aunt Boo said to herself: "Nothing tastes better than a warm bowl of soup on a cold winter's night."

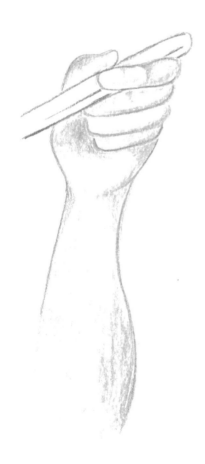

"What was that? Did I hear something in the attic?"

Aunt Boo went back to stirring her soup. Then she heard it again.

"I know it's something coming from the attic. What can it be?"

"A mouse? They are always getting inside the house when winter sets in. It sounds like tiny feet running across the floor."

"It's too late tonight. I will check out the attic tomorrow."

In his hide-away, Scamper found one of Aunt Boo's favorite quilts and settled down for the evening.

The next morning, Aunt Boo went to the entrance to the attic and pulled the staircase down. She slowly crept up the stairs.

She reached up and pulled the dangling light string. The attic burst into light.

Aunt Boo looked across the room. In the corner, Scamper was playing hide-and-seek, jumping in and out of a box.

The room was a mess. Scamper had eaten all the pecans and scattered the broken shells everywhere.

"I might have known it would be you," Aunt Boo said.

Grabbing an old umbrella, she rushed toward Scamper shouting, "Get out of here, you pest! I love my animals, but I can't have you living in my attic."

Scamper, confused, ran
toward the escape hole
and squeezed out as
fast as he could.

Back he ran and
climbed into the hole
in the old oak tree.

Scamper
lay quietly.
He was
exhausted
and drifted
off to sleep.

Aunt Boo's handyman came the next morning.

"Something must be done," she said to the man.

"I can't have that mischievous squirrel Scamper living in my house."

"We will see about the hole and seal it for good," said the handyman.

Scamper's hide-away was forever sealed, but Scamper never knew it.

Scamper was up the next morning and headed for the trellis beside the house. Aunt Boo was sweeping off the patio, and he decided not to bother her.

Scamper climbed up the trellis and headed toward his hide-away. He looked and looked for the entrance.

It had to be there someplace.

Scamper finally gave up and ran back into the rain gutter.

Aunt Boo kept sweeping. Suddenly a noise came from the rain gutter. Aunt Boo heard a running rumble above her head.

"Now who do you suppose that is?" she said to herself.

Aunt Boo swung her broom upward and rapped three times on the rain gutter. Scamper came flying straight up into the air.

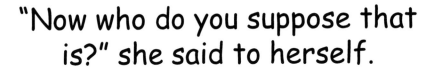

That was the end of the secret hide-away in Aunt Boo's attic for Scamper.

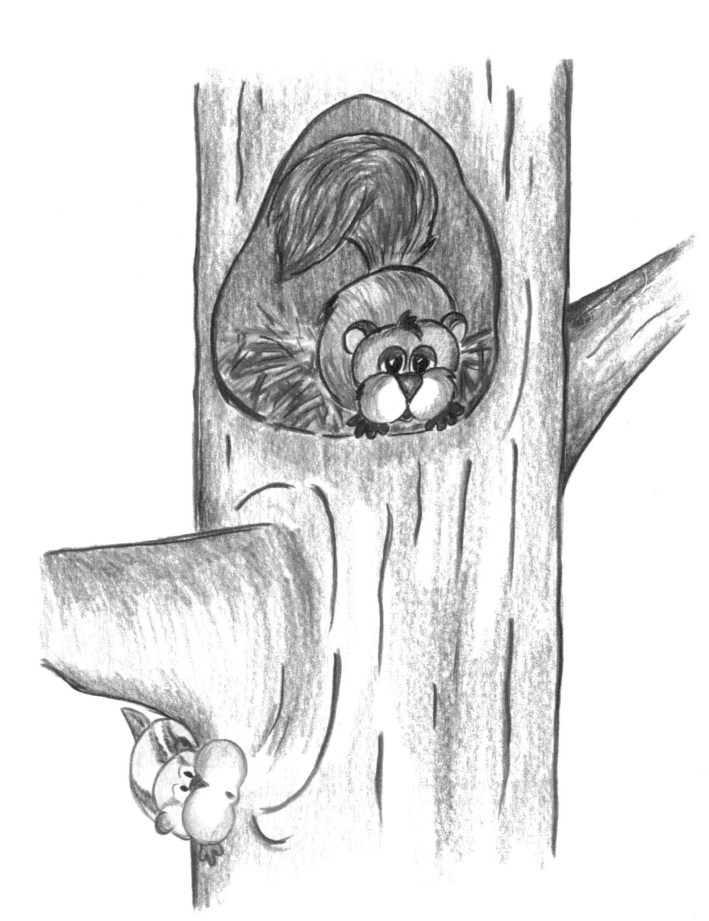

Follow the adventures of Scamper, the Mischievous Squirrel, as he discovers snow and Christmas decorations.

Coming in Winter 2011.

About the Author

Patricia Eytcheson Taylor met her first husband, John, on the beaches of southern California, where she grew up. Her mother was very ill, and her father made sure she had plenty of animals to give her love and comfort. Pat learned to understand and communicate with the animals, making it easy for her to tell their stories when she became a writer. She is not only the author of the Scamper, the Mischievous Squirrel stories, but she is also the model for Aunt Boo, and the stories are based on her own experiences with a mischievous squirrel. She wrote three acclaimed children's books about the horse Catch a Winner. After being widowed for several years, she married the Reverend James C. Taylor, an Army chaplain, and together they co-authored a Christian living book, *On the Wings of the Wind*.

About the Illustrator

Nancy Garnett Peterson grew up in Shelley, Idaho, on a small acreage with four brothers and plenty of chores. At the age of fourteen she raised her own cattle to help pay for college. After attending Boise State University, marrying a pilot, having three children, and moving to Texas, she began her career as an illustrator. Houston would introduce her to a few authors (no cattle) and launch her publishing career; she currently has eleven books published. Texas is her home, but her creative mind still wanders back to her childhood Snake River Valley. She often ventures out West where she enjoys art lessons and hugs with her four granddaughters and only grandson.

CPSIA information can be obtained
at www.ICGtesting.com
Printed in the USA
246681LV00004B